Dinner Party Music

Adam Greenfield

BAMBOO DART PRESS

LOS ANGELES † NEW YORK † LONDON † MELBOURNE

Dinner Party Music by Adam Greenfield
978-1-962316-03-3 Paperback
978-1-962316-04-0 eBook

Cover artwork by Abby Weintraub
Layout and design by Mark Givens

For information:
Bamboo Dart Press
chapbooks@bamboodartpress.com

Bamboo Dart Press 050

Pelekinesis
www.pelekinesis.com

BAMBOO DART PRESS
www.bamboodartpress.com

SHRIMPER
www.shrimperrecords.com

Back when I was much, much younger, before my mother walked out the door, never to return, I used to like to sit in the kitchen, watching cartoons after school and smearing huge dabs of Rondelé cheese onto Ritz Crackers. It was the height of luxury and I knew it.

I felt a shiver run through me with each bite, and when the *GI Joe* theme song would play when the show returned from commercials, it was almost too much to bear. Sensory overload, but of the best kind. Like being waterboarded in custard.

I knew how good I had it.

The door opened and the smell of night jasmine, blooming just as the sun was starting to set, leached in, coating everything in its alien candy scent, sticky and delicious, like too good to be true. I wanted to eat it by the bucketful, suck it up through a straw, spoon it over myself in bas-relief.

"Close your eyes, sweetheart." It was my mother. Her voice was warm, rich, always so full of grace and forgiveness whether you needed it or not. I started to turn, but she put her arms on me from behind and gently stopped me. Her hands, soft and light, covered my eyes so I couldn't see anything. "Close your eyes," she said again.

This time I did it.

The night Grandpa Al disappeared, it was just me, Dad and him in the house. Cam, my younger brother, was still a month away from being kicked out of his house by Bonnie, who was sick of his temper tantrums. During one of our infrequent calls, he told me that she'd filed six restraining orders against him.

"Jesus," I'd responded, lost in the wonder of that number, "that's enough to make a jacket out of."

"What is wrong with you, Vaughn?" he'd asked, and I could hear the anger in his voice, the inability to accept this much difference in anyone or anything. "You are just as dumb as you've ever been, aren't you?"

He was younger than me by about two years, but he was always the one in charge. Ever since he came out he'd had nothing but disdain for me, a morbid somberness, like every time we spoke he was at a séance having a conversation with the dead. Cam was angry like Dad and it made him seem much older than me. More broken down. I guess if I had to choose then I'd choose being a tad slow in the brains department if it meant I wasn't so ground down looking. It looked exhausting.

Anyway, this was right before he came back, when it was just me, Dad, Uncle Bert and Grandpa Al. We all lived together in a giant house that had been in the family for generations. Grandma Flora had left years ago. Right out the same door as Mom. Just left one day and never came back. They say Grandpa was never the same since, but I find it hard to believe he hadn't always been an angry prick. He seemed born to it.

The bedrooms of the house unfurled in every direction from central hallways on the first and second floors. All you had to do was follow the path and you'd wind up in a room that had a bed and a dresser, a closet and a few old oil paintings of dubious origins, all having to do with the sea, a condition that had no relation to this family, whatsoever, that I knew of. All those sea paintings used to make me feel self-conscious, like we were trying to claim someone else's notion of a legacy; a real way to be.

Until she left, Mom was the only woman in the house and I could see how it wore on her. I probably spent more time with her than anyone else. You didn't have to be a genius to know I was Mom's favorite. She hated the whole anger thing. Absolutely disdained it. She thought my dad, uncle, grandpa and even Cam were ridiculous the way they were always carrying on. She might've been able to stand it, if she'd gotten it, but she never understood how these men could get so bent out of shape over the stupidest shit. I'm sure there'd been a time when she politely avoided Grandpa Al and his "tiny tirades" as we called them, backed out of the kitchen if Uncle Bert was in there, trying to get the lid off a jar of pickles, swearing and spitting as he twisted and twisted. "A stroke waiting to happen" I'd heard her say to Dad, and even though I didn't know what a stroke was exactly, I knew he wasn't well and that there was only so much a body could take. She even let Dad rant and rave, which was how his anger came out, swearing about some politician on the news and then looking at her like she was the crazy one. She caught a lot of this kind of shrapnel, and I saw how it wore holes in her, left dents in her skin and on her heart.

And then there was Cam, probably the last hope in her mind, but that didn't turn out so well. Cam was tension personified, a single-muscled organism looking for a reason to contract. He could have been a world class athlete if he wasn't such a monster, all that rage always looking for an outlet, or really more a place to connect. Something to plug into. Thank god he never had a cause - he would have been unstoppable.

I don't know when she first had the idea to leave, but it wasn't exactly an unknown quantity in the house. All the women had left; Grandma Flora, Aunt Helen, Aunt Louise, cousins and siblings, married and spinster alike. I'd never met any of them, but you could almost see a path worn on the kitchen floor leading to the back door. I'd heard about them all, seen pictures, heard stories, and they created little whirlpools in each of the men they were closest to. Not enough to suck you down, but enough to trap you for a good long while.

"I wonder if it's something about that door, that they all keep leaving," Dad had said to me one night, a cigarette burning low between two crooked fingers, which trembled all the time now. It was one of the only ways I knew for sure he was still here, sometimes, late at night in the stillness of the kitchen, when he would stare all the time, and he just looked paper thin, a see-through version of himself. The trembling fingers told me he was still real. I suppose I could have touched him, but that didn't occur to me back then.

He had a point about the door. That's a lot of women leaving and you'd be crazy if you didn't at least *contemplate* the notion of a curse or a monster. Some crazy-eyed, shambling beast that roamed the halls, eaten away by remorse.

"Are you sure you saw her walk out..." he sucked on the cigarette and then let the smoke slowly trickle out over his lips. He pointed, "...that door?"

"Yes." I nodded.

Even though I'd told him a million times since that day that I saw her walk out the door, the truth was, I couldn't be a 100% sure. I was ninety nine percent sure, which felt close enough to 100% to stand for something, but there was that one percent... I decided I could keep that 1% for myself, though. It felt like it was the least I could do, a little mysterious gift I could take out and ponder when life got too sure of itself.

I wanted it to be a hundred, and I wondered if it was something in the way I answered the question, ringing in my ears for 30 years now, that made him feel like he had to ask again and again, or if he just needed to keep hearing it, keep being reminded as though he were emerging from a decades long coma each day and getting caught up on the news. Whatever the case, I never complained. It wasn't in my nature and I didn't know what good it would do, anyway. I just answered, again and again, until I didn't even know what the question meant anymore, or if he was even talking to me.

"Yes."

"Close your eyes."

Mom's voice said on that flawless glass sculpture of a day. She leaned in close and I got another nose full of that jasmine. Something inside me clicked over, like an odometer turning over from 999,999 back to 0, and I felt my senses slip into a perfect harmony with one another. Between the cartoons, my mouth cemented shut with a clot of moistened cheese and crackers, and now this smell, I felt like I was filled up to the top with something pure, something golden, and it would soon be overflowing out of me, and maybe I'd look golden, too.

"No, no," she said, keeping her hand over my eyes, "you have to keep them closed. If you keep them closed, I'll tell you a secret. Would you like that?"

I squirmed in my seat. A secret on top of everything else? Secrets were my second favorite thing in the world. It went: magic, secrets, wishes and then games. In that order.

I nodded vigorously, still trying to swallow the mush in my mouth.

"Okay," she said, gingerly taking her hands away. "But after I tell you the secret you have to stay here until you hear the back door close. Okay?"

There was something in her voice, something far behind the cheerfulness she was trying to lead with, that sounded worried and sad, but the secret had me intrigued and I ignored the other stuff, just as she knew I would, agreeing right away to her demands with the utmost enthusiasm.

"Promise?" she asked.

"Promise!" I almost screamed, ready to get to the good part.

She laughed. "Vaughn, Vaughn, Vaughn..."

"Mom, Mom, Mom..." I parroted back at her, and she laughed again, but this time I thought I heard her laugh get caught up on a bubble in her throat, a sob maybe, or exhaustion.

She turned the TV off and the room was plunged into a sudden silence that unnerved me, that made me feel like loneliness could be a place.

"Mom?" I asked tentatively, my eyes still sealed shut.

"I'm still here, Vaughn."

"What's the secret?"

Another pause. Looking back, I can only imagine what she was thinking, how she was still trying to piece together how she wanted to say what she told me next.

"Vaughn, listen to me," her voice was low, like a whisper, and I couldn't tell exactly where she was standing. "There are people living in the walls of this house. I hear them talking at night, sometimes crying. The worst of all is when they're laughing. I thought it was just my imagination at first, but I don't think so anymore."

I heard her footsteps and then felt the hem of her dress scrape against my leg as she walked past and it sent shivers through me so it felt like I had superpowers. I could tell she was wearing fancy shoes by the way they tapped as she walked and I wondered if she was planning on going out later. She didn't wear dresses and fancy shoes except when she and Daddy were going out to dinner with friends. That meant chicken pot pies for me and Cam, which was okay by me, because chicken pot pies were my favorite food in the whole wide world.

"When you and Cam are at school and your dad's at work I sit here and listen to them. It's hard to make out what they're saying, but I try. I listen so hard, but it never quite makes sense. Sometimes I ask them what they want, but they only laugh. I used to think they were making fun of me, but lately I've been starting to think they're not sure who they are or how they got here." She took a deep breath and when she let it out, nice and slow, I could hear how tired and scared she was. "But I know who they are."

I heard her walk a few more steps and then open the door. The smell of jasmine bounded in like an over-eager puppy, and for the first time in my life I wished it didn't. It was covering up the smell of her perfume and I was afraid for it to leave me, already sensing that there wasn't much time left.

"That's not the secret, though. The secret is…are you ready for the secret?"

I nodded, but I wasn't sure I was ready. I wasn't sure I wanted to know the secret anymore.

"The secret is that you don't have to be one of them," her voice was trailing off, getting harder and harder to hear, like she was fading out. "The secret is that you're not like them."

It was starting to feel like something wasn't right. I wanted to take my hands away from my face, to open my eyes, let the sunlight flash back in, race to Mom, hug her, beg her to keep me safe from the men in the walls, but I didn't. I made a promise.

She was just standing there in the doorway. I could feel her thinking about the great, big world, sizing it up, maybe even getting close to 1 after counting backwards from some impossibly huge number. A googolplex. Infinity.

And then, without any warning, the door closed and there was the familiar rattle of the blinds clattering against the little window in the frame, a sound that I used to love, because it meant someone was just getting home. But when I opened my eyes, she was gone.

"Mom?" I called out, already feeling like something was wrong, that she hadn't just stepped out, but that she was gone. It was just something I felt. The kitchen felt different to me, suddenly, hollowed out, empty in a way that places feel that have long since been abandoned.

"Mom?" I said again, and the tears started to fall. My hands fell away from my face.

And then, from the wall right next to the door, I heard what sounded like laughter.

I got up and moved toward the spot and reached out my hand, slowly, to touch it. I expected heat, tingling, maybe even that my hand would go right through and come out the other side, but there was none of that. It was just a wall.

Then I heard the laughter again and I knew for sure I wasn't just hearing things. It was coming from inside the wall, from that spot right next to the door. At first it was just one laugh, but the longer I stayed there, the day outside turning slowly and softly to night, more voices joined in, so that by the time Dad came home from work, there were dozens of them, a mountain of laughter, one piled on top of the other, reaching uselessly into the sky like a pagan relic.

I was slumped against the wall, my ear glued to it, when Dad came in. He saw me, dropped his briefcase, and immediately looked back through the door he'd just come, looking for her, I supposed, already understanding that it'd happened again. Maybe he was surprised that it'd finally happened to him, but, as he took me by the shoulders, I saw in his eyes, dulled already by sadness, that he knew it had always been a matter of time.

"Are you sure she went out the door? Are you 100% sure that's where she went?"

At first, I just looked at him. It was like I couldn't understand what he was saying, like his words were muffled, coming from inside the wall. But after a few minutes, I understood what it was he wanted. He wasn't asking me anything. He knew I could hear them. He knew that I knew who they were. And I think what he was asking me was if there was room in there for him.

So I did what I could to help him. "Yes," I answered for the first time of a million.

"Yes."

The next nine years passed in what felt like one endless day. We spent those years playing a cataclysmic game of hide and seek that was all hiders and no seekers, the five of us, doing all we could to disappear into ourselves and the threadbare lives we'd made while passing the time.

For the most part, Dad spent his days sitting at the kitchen table watching the back door, drinking Coors from the can and clearing his throat a lot, like he was getting ready to say something. But nothing ever came out.

Grandpa wandered in and out of the kitchen at regular intervals, but never stayed long. Whenever I'd catch him he'd always look around like he wasn't quite sure where he was or how he got there. I think his confusion was genuine, but in those days it was hard to tell for sure. Nothing felt real and there were shadows everywhere. No matter how we had the lights positioned, or if the shades were open or closed, we were overrun by slivers of darkness, weird shapes metastasizing along the floors and walls and ceiling, crawling all over the place like a plague of insects.

Cam wasn't around much in those days, choosing to spend most of his time playing after school games of street football. He'd come home about seven, bruised and bleeding, and demand to be fed. Dad obliged with the least amount of effort, serving up TV dinners and other frozen crap he'd dump on the table in front of us. I'd always be sure to thank him, but

Cam never did. He'd just tear through the food and then either run back outside for more bare-knuckle bonding or up to his room where he blasted his Metallica tapes, willing himself to go supernova with the greatest of ease.

I did my best to stay out of everyone's way, choosing to leave my room only after Dad had finally drunk so much beer that his eyes started to cross and spin around, like he'd just gotten bonked in a Looney Tunes. Once the coast was clear, I liked to come down to the kitchen and listen at the walls. Get down on the ground real low and put my ear right up against it. I loved being in that position. It felt so good to be huddled right next to the wall, but not going in it. I didn't hear anything at first, but I believed what Mom said, because she'd seemed so sad about the people she heard in there. If she'd been teasing me the day she left, I would have heard the smile in her voice, and also, she would have told me. *Otherwise*, she'd said to me one of those dreamy days, *it's lying*.

Uncle Bert was still around then and he walked in on me a couple of times. He never said much, even when he caught me down on the floor on my hands and knees, trying to hear what the voices were saying, trying to trace the hairline cracks that seemed to be expanding every time I went back, and I couldn't figure out if it was the house that was moving or if it was the way I was looking at things. Both possibilities seemed equally plausible.

One night I didn't hear him come in and then suddenly his voice was coming at me from all sides at once, like fucking demons in terry cloth robes with nothing on underneath; venal.

"If you listen real close you can hear them sons of bitches frolicking at the beach." It shook me to the core, that sound, and I screamed. "You're not going to hear them until it's time. And then when it's time," he laughed a little and then stopped suddenly, "then it's just a matter of time."

"They're not just in the kitchen, you know. They're everywhere. All over the house. But I think this is where you have to go in. This spot right here next to the door." He pointed at that part of the wall. "Poetic justice, that." He stood there sipping one of Dad's beers, staring at that spot on the wall like it was a pin-up. I was too afraid to move, like if I'd stood up or said something he would've gotten pulled right in. It felt inevitable, and I think he felt it, too. "I hope you never turn into one of these guys, sitting around the kitchen, waiting for your wife to come back. They're never coming."

"I know that," I said, a sixteen year old virgin who didn't know much, couldn't know much, but who knew that. Felt it, like the blood in me.

He patted me on the shoulder and we never talked again, because two weeks later, I saw him go right into that wall, not unhappily, flipping me the bird with both hands as he went.

When Dad came home from work that night, I was waiting at the table, chomping at the bit to tell him about it.

"Uncle Bert left today," I said, pointing at the wall, more than a little curious to see what he'd say.

He followed the arc of my finger and sighed.

"Wall or door?" he asked.

"Wall," I said, a little amazed that he knew and had never said anything before.

"Figures," he said, not really talking to me or himself, but just talking, feeding back into the room like a machine tuned to the wrong frequency.

I was back in the house after being gone for ten years, fresh out of a two-year marriage and wretched with thoughts of Roslyn. We met four years ago at one of those bars up on Sunset that catered to lonely people who liked to drink within spitting distance of a mechanical bull. I was up there, waving my arms and moving around the saddle, trying to look like the male version of Debra Winger in *Urban Cowboy*, because to me, that was the sexiest thing I'd ever seen anyone ever do with their body in my whole life. When I looked down I saw this pretty blonde with a cowboy hat watching me through a tall glass of something brown. She was smiling, and I thought she looked as innocent as fruit.

After I got bucked off we talked for awhile and then we went out to the parking lot and started making out next to her old Suzuki Samurai that she babied like it was a fawn.

"You're for me," she said, coming up for air between these fathomless, open-mouthed kisses. Kisses I knew that might rip the soul out of me, but that I kept going back for. "I knew it when I looked up there and saw you on that bull."

"You sure about that?" I asked, worried about getting trapped under an avalanche of cowboy fantasies I'd never be able to dig my way out of. "Everything looks great when you look at it through a glass of Jim Beam. All golden like that. It's…,"

"What?" she said, and I could see her tongue coming back in for another round, ready to swoop in and mow me down like that crop duster in *North By Northwest.*

I kicked at the imaginary dirt at my feet. Wishing for acres of undiscovered land to spoil with her. "It can be a lot to live up to. That's all I'm saying."

"Don't try to unsell me," she said, grabbing me again and pulling me in close.

"I'm just being honest," I told her. "You could fall in love with a stop sign looking at it through all that gold."

"I'm not interested in honesty, silly boy..." she laughed as she threaded her lips back onto mine, kissing me harder than I'd ever been kissed before. I wanted her to finish her sentence, to find out what it was that did interest her, but I never did. Even after the end.

We lasted four years before she threw me out. I loved her a lot, and knew that I'd miss her, but I didn't argue. Growing up how I did, with all those ways out of our house and one another's lives, the one thing I learned was you can't argue with people when they get like that. Personally, I didn't think that made me dumb. I thought it made me kind of smart.

When I moved back home the voices were much louder than they were before I'd left. I'd been gone years, but somehow they knew all about me. I could hear them gossiping in there, laughing, clinking glasses, and I was sure they were talking about me. About how my marriage hadn't lasted and how I didn't have a job, and to my ears, they didn't sound like they were all that surprised.

Grandpa was next to go, and when it finally came, I kind of wondered what had taken so long. Dad and I had fallen into a sort of rhythm of sitting at the kitchen table, him with his beers and me with my Jameson, a couple of soused statues passing time, whole days that drew their tempo from the worn out circuitry of the house. We had the paper on the table between us, the sports page was always half-heartedly opened to the box scores of whatever sport was in season, but we weren't really looking at that. We were looking at the wall and the door, hypnotized by them, maybe a little in awe.

Grandpa came into the kitchen wearing the see-through robe he favored and the slippers that smelled like the 70's.

"Will one of you get me my cigarettes?" he asked, and when I got up to get them Dad got up, too. He had to pee. As soon as we turned the corner, though, we heard this loud *POP* and then a slurping sound that was kind of hard to describe, kind of a wet sucking like the last breath you take before you drown, the one where you get your first mouthful of water and you know it's gonna be your last.

We stopped in our tracks and looked at one another. Then we turned around and ran into the kitchen, but it was already too late. Grandpa was gone and the wall was shimmering a little like it didn't want to be there, and then suddenly it was back. There was no sound, no marks on the wall, just one of Grandpa's fuzzy slippers sitting right next to it, like it'd just slipped off his foot and he'd be right back to get it. Dad picked it up and looked at it, turning it over in his hands this way and that.

He walked right up to the wall and whispered. "Dad?" Then I heard his voice break apart a little, not quite crying, but as close as he could still get. "Daddy?"

After that, we were at that table all the time. We even went to the bathroom in shifts so that we wouldn't miss a thing. We never talked about it, but it was pretty clear what we were doing there. It felt like waiting, but it wasn't. We were stalking something. Something we knew that was dangerous and would probably eat us alive, but inevitable also, so why not get it out of the way? Also, neither of us had anywhere better to be. We were meeting our fate head on.

We drank a lot over the next two months before Cam came home. Hard drinking. Mean, quiet drinking. But we never raised our voices to one another. That was probably mostly because the voices in the wall had gotten louder by then – Grandpa had never been what you'd call a shrinking violet – but still, I was proud of us for that.

Dad's birthday was looming, and while it wasn't 70, 65 still had a certain litigious weight to it. It felt like a bureaucrat's age, the age when you started winding it all down.

I tried to talk to him to get his mind off everything, about Grandpa, but he wasn't really having it. Between sips of beer he rhapsodized - mostly too himself, I realized – confirming every nasty suspicion he'd ever had about the man and vaguely smug that by going into the wall he'd finally been proven right. Abandonment, anger…it was a wretched description of the human condition and I didn't begrudge him a second of it. In fact, I sometimes uttered words of encouragement, pithy little affirmations befitting a little league coach. "You can do this!" "That's right!" None of it rolled off the tongue, and if it did, it rolled right into the gutter, dirtying itself with the ass-licking of pandering to an unrepentant narcissist.

I found out that Cam was coming back one night when his wife, Bonnie, called me out of the blue. She was full of rage, collapsing under an avalanche of bullshit and ultimatums.

"Vaughn, it's Bonnie. I just threw Cam out. We're done. He's probably on his way over to you now. Vaughn," my sister-in-law went on, "I am so sorry it's taken me this long to tell you what an absolute idiot I think you are. I'm sorry we haven't had the chance to talk about it. But me and Roslyn see each other sometimes. We go up to that rodeo bar on Sunset where you two met and she tells me funny stories about how she thought you were being ironic for ten years but it turned out that really you were just a jackass."

I wasn't sure what she wanted. On the off chance it was forgiveness she wanted she could certainly have it.

"Fuck it, Bonnie. Let bygones be bygones. Besides, I've got bigger fish to fry! There's this wall in the kitchen..."

She started yelling again, not waiting for me to finish.

"You're not listening, moron! I'm done. Done with your whole weird family. You, your sad dad and especially your passive aggressive brother who needs more medication than he can afford. The craziest thing is, you're the sweetest of the bunch. But that doesn't mean anything. You know that, right? At the end of the day."

"I know," I said, happy to be an accomplice to her catharsis.

"Anyway, you can tell your fucked up brother that he's not fingering his way out of this one! Got me?" She started laughing. "All you guys living in that house together. You'd think one of you..."

She went silent and I felt a shiver run through me. I wanted to know what she was going to say. What piece of information she had for me. This was human intelligence. The best kind.

"What?" I asked. "Say it."

It was quiet for another few seconds and then she hung up. She either didn't have the words or maybe it was that it was too sad to say.

I wasn't surprised that Cam came was coming home. Not because it felt inevitable or anything cosmic or country-fried like that, but because it came when it did, right after Grandpa had gone. Even if Bonnie hadn't thrown him out, I was sure he'd be coming back. It was like he was called here. The house was full of places where bodies used to be. It craved them, the smell of them, their shadows. It might be made of bodies, or was a body itself, living and dreaming with wants all its own. In any event, Cam came back, and he was shot out of a fucking cannon.

We were sitting at the kitchen table, Dad with the business section of the *Times* and me with an old copy of *Consumer Reports* from 1991 I found lying around. Cam looked at us, his big duffel by his feet, and I could tell he wanted to spit on the ground or punch out a cop or do something that he could get arrested for but also put on his resume.

"What're you two doing just sitting there staring at the wall?" He was nasty, offended to his core. "I don't want to start in with this bad luck shit again. I know you think there's a curse or a monster or something, but believe me, the only fucking curse around here is your attitude." He was pointing at Dad. Pointing through him. "And then," his finger swung to me, "you bring this one into it. You know how he is. You know he'll go along with whatever you tell him."

I really wanted to know what he meant by "you know how

this one is" but I held it in and tried to calm him down, leading him by the shoulders into the next room.

"You've got to be calmer. Be nicer to him. He's about to be 65."

Cam looked at me as seriously as I've ever been looked at and then, barely suppressing the anger that seethed through him, he said, "Who gives a fucking shit?" And then his eyes narrowed at me, gilding me in shame. "You're not buying this wall shit, are you? Jesus, Vaughn."

I was shocked and pulled back a little.

Dad was down to about four hours of sleep a night and I knew he relied on me to stay awake in case anything happened with the wall. "You think you're the only one who's seen things? Heard things?" He went on, livid, and I could see how well he had this laid out in his mind, how this was the absolute truth of the matter. "There are no people in the walls!" He pointed violently at the wall, to the great unwashed masses, our ancestors, rubes and bullies all. "You didn't hear any of that yourself! You heard them – Grandpa and Dad and Uncle Bert - you heard them and you believed it. Those three guys! They were crazy! Men shouldn't live together like this. It's not natural. Of course they were out of their minds." Then he came down from his anger, and I saw all the energy drain from his face, and he became flushed with sadness and slowness, a deadly kind of quiet which is when you're at your heaviest. "And you always believed all their stories."

I got real frozen inside, all of a sudden, and I thought about it. I knew what I'd seen. The only thing I cared about was that Dad was next and I wasn't quite ready to let that happen. I knew for *sure* Cam wasn't. Even though he was always fed up with the man, he absolutely worshipped him. They were the same person holding two ends of a live wire.

"How about all those women leaving?"

He waved it away like it was yesterday's news. That part didn't bother him and I had no idea why. He just didn't think about Mom much. She was like an organ he didn't need. If I was cavalier about the whole thing, I'd say that I was jealous, but that wasn't even close to the truth. I was fine with the memories. They didn't all have to make you cry.

The one nice thing Cam did for me when he moved back in was to bring me a really nice bottle of Irish whiskey, an affliction for which he knew me to have a desperate predilection.

I eyed the buxom green bottle suspiciously when he pulled it out of his rucksack and handed it over, like he was paying some medieval toll to cross a bridge.

"Don't worry," he said, his voice was suffused with a baby-faced slyness that made my skin crawl. "It ain't poisoned."

With Dad's birthday rapidly approaching, it felt like it was only a matter of time now before he went. It wasn't a question of being pessimistic. It just felt inevitable now, the way you knew the roof would one day start to leak or the smoke detector would start buzzing in the dreamiest, softest part of the night. Nothing changed with Cam being back, and pretty soon he was at the table with us with an old copy of *Penthouse Forum* that had passed between us hundreds of times growing up and that I not only knew by heart, but was the foundation of my sexual identity. I'd expected sex to be so much more literary than it'd turned out to be, dirtier and more verbose, and always narrated by a creep of the highest order, the restraining order champion of the world.

We were almost like a little family again, and one night after Indian take out, I started humming a tune. It was something from the past that just came to me.

It struck a nerve with Dad and he put his paper down, took off his glasses and looked over at me. He had a smile on his face – the first one I'd seen in what felt like years – and I smiled back as I felt every muscle in my body suddenly go tight with love.

"That tune..." he started to say, and I realized it'd been a long time since I last heard him speak, days maybe, and I'd started wondering if maybe he was out of words, like how at the end of your life, you run out of breath. "I know that tune."

I stopped and put the magazine down. "You do?"

"Yes. I think your mother used to play it. On the piano. Or hum it."

I'd forgotten Mom used to play the piano, or that she was always humming some little tune until he said it and it made me wonder what else I'd forgotten about her.

"Maybe..." I said, wrapping my knuckles against the side of

my head, biting my lower lip, performing all those little sadomasochistic rituals we do to punish ourselves for not remembering what we spent lifetimes trying to forget.

His face was flushed with color and he looked rosy, reanimated, risen from his perpetual end.

"Your mother's favorite kind of music was dinner party music," he pointed a crooked finger at me, and I could see him filling up with the memory as the tune grew louder in his head. "That's what she called it, too. Dinner party music." He guffawed.

Cam and I shot glances at one another, a couple of skeptical duelists. This was new territory and neither one of us was sure whether we should be calling 911 or if it was truly a good thing.

"'But that's not music,' I tried to tell her," Dad went on, turning his head to gaze at the kitchen door, his eyes filled with something like compassion, like he was seeing it for the first time and it was just a door, after all. "'It's air' I tried to tell her. 'It's the atmosphere.' But she didn't care. She just laughed at me. 'That can be music, too, silly Billy. Can't you see that?'" It wasn't clear to me if he was talking to himself or to me and Cam, but regardless, we nodded along, happy to be complicit in his pantomime.

He looked down at the table and shook his head, not to break the spell, I thought, but because he wanted to go in deeper, down into this dream of his; past his shoulders, feel it tickle his neck as it rose rose rose...now warm against his chin, now to his lips that should have known when to stop talking, and finally up past his nose he turned up at her silliness, at the fact that someone's favorite kind of music could be dinner party music. He wouldn't be done until his lungs were filled up with it. It was the thing he wanted to do him in, to let that melody slowly suffocate him, to die a symphony.

"But she didn't care. She loved her *La De Dah* music." Then, he did something I don't think either of us had ever seen before. He started singing. And he wasn't just singing, he was belting it out, crooning actually, and I wanted so badly to sing along with him, and was about to join in, when, from out of the wall, a chorus of male voices started in, who knows how many generations of snappy dressers and bad husbands, humming along to a tune they all remembered but not a one of them could place.

I looked at Cam and he looked back at me and just kind of shrugged. He started drumming his fingers on the table, keeping time like any younger brother whose holy job would always be to be a perpetual motion machine. I was surprised to find that I myself was whistling. Me! Not a musical bone... But here I was and here we were. The karaoke of the damned, I thought, and I wanted to say it, because I knew how loud everyone would laugh and how long they'd remember it and bring it up over Indian food take out 50 years from now, but I didn't want to stop the song. That felt like it would be a terrible thing to do.

"*Dee Dee Dum...*" Dad kept going, and he looked really unstoppable, almost invincible, or maybe just not so tragic for once, which felt like the same thing. He was swaying, too, and I couldn't tell if he was conducting the music or if he was dancing to it or if there was even a difference and what did it really fucking matter? Lost was lost. What difference did it matter, how lost?

...and we were a symphony, all of us together, marshalled by grief, howling our simple, excruciating truths.

And then, just as it was feeling like we were getting to the top of something, that point where you can see out to forever, but more importantly perhaps, that there was nothing else above you to look down on you. Just when we'd gotten to that place there was this scratching sound at the back door, and in a moment like the Big Bang, all the voices fell away and it was just the three of us again, serenading an old door, with an old song, a wordless tune we all knew by heart.

Dad got there first. I'd never seen him move so fast in my life. He was brushing over his thinning hair with one hand while he yanked the door open with the other, and we couldn't see past him, but you'd have to be crazy to think that there wasn't just a small part of me that thought it might be my mother. Just one small, little boy speck of a thing that imagined the thing we'd just been doing was magical somehow, or at least as magical as a wall that pulled men of my family into it, and maybe. Just maybe...

Dad was already screaming when I got around him. I really thought it was going to be Mom. It felt that it had to be her, that nothing else made sense.

But it wasn't her, and I felt instantly ashamed of myself, but then sobered up when I saw what was there. An opossum. A big, thick, nightmare of a thing with a face that looked like it was doing an impression of a man. It wasn't moving, startled, I assumed, by the sudden burst of light and by this natural disaster of a voice that was suddenly drilling into its very essence, its fucking thoughtless core. Honestly, I was kind of worried Dad was going to stamp on it. Smear its guts all over the fucking place and I really didn't have the stomach for that. Luckily, it quickly regained its senses and ran off in a zig-zagging pattern, leaving Cam and I kind of mesmerized, watching it disappear into the darkness.

That wasn't good enough for Dad, though. He'd had it. He kept on yelling after it, chasing it into the darkness with his voice.

"That's not music!" he screamed into the night. "You think dinner party music is real music, but it's not! And it never will be!" His index finger was going up and then down. Up then down. He was at the Hague, he was Norma Rae. He was indignant and would not hear reason. A few dogs started barking a retort and he yelled back. "Dinner party music? No one ever heard of that! That's not a thing! Everyone knows that's not a thing!" He was our spokesman, whether we needed one or not.

I ran upstairs and grabbed the bottle of Green Spot Cam had brought me that sat on top of my dresser, and hauled ass back to the kitchen. Before I could find a glass, Dad grabbed the bottle out of my hand and hoisted it to his lips. He drank without stopping, slowly bending backwards like a paler St.

Louis Arch as the whiskey poured down his throat. He looked like a building about to fall and he showed no signs of stopping, I realized, as his Adam's apple bobbed up and down and I couldn't even be sure if he was breathing anymore, if that was even a thing he still needed to do. He leaned back further, and further still, as the liquor splashed all over his heart and I could swear I heard his bones creaking the way they say you can hear bamboo growing in those forests in China. Only he wasn't growing. He wasn't even trying to get drunk. He was trying to break himself in half, I understood, astonished by his flexibility. He didn't want to be whole anymore.

"Dad. Dad, you should slow down. You're going to fall." I looked over at Cam for help, but his lower jaw was hanging open, his eyes saucer wide. "Do something," I hissed. "He's going to hurt himself."

"It's like 9/11 all over again," Cam said, his voice all marbled with awe.

Cam used to compare a lot of things to 9/11, too many, honestly, and when I said something to him about it once he told me he was at work on acid when it all went down. Knowing a little about a person can go a long way sometimes. Brick by brick we are our facts.

I grabbed the bottle out of Dad's hands, but he fought me for it, and then Cam was there helping me and we wrestled it away from him. After a few seconds he stopped struggling and he let us hold him. Just the three of us, quiet in a way that felt good, swaying and grasping on to one another, relief flowing through us. When a line of snot shot from his nose and hung in a state of suspended mortification halfway to the floor, I grabbed it the way I'd seen parents do for their sniveling brats and flung it towards the kitchen sink, my first paternal instinct rearing its impotent little head.

Dad reared back and squinched his face up at me.

"What is wrong with you?" he shouted.

Honestly, I didn't know what he was talking about. I wasn't sure if he was talking about the thing with the snot, and I was going to say something untrue like, *You'd do the same from me*, but he turned on Cam without getting his answer, and asked him the same thing.

"What is wrong with you?"

This time it was a softer question, though, a little more desperate, asking us perhaps, I realized in my slow way, the thing he was too scared to ask himself.

"Shh...shh," I whispered, wrapping him in a hug and patting his back, hoping I was doing the right thing, wondering if there was even a right thing to do in a situation like this. Cam came in, too, and Dad finally stopped struggling and let us hold him. He went boneless and we were holding him up between us; we were his spine, his arms, his aching head. It was probably the first time in his life that he'd ever let himself go like this, and I hoped it felt good to let himself die just a little.

We'd been in the kitchen pretty much around the clock since the thing with the possum. We were starting to feel like doomsday preppers, huddled at the table in our unwashed blankets, unshaven, staring blankly at the wall where it felt like at any moment something was going to crash into us from outer space. A few empty tins of sardines sat on the table. We didn't even have our reading material anymore. There was no more pretending we were just biding our time. We were firmly in the realm of inevitability and the depths of it were unfathomable.

Every once in awhile I'd sneak a look at Dad just to make sure he was still there. He barely made a sound, except to lift his hand out from under his blanket now and then to scratch his nose, and sometimes I'd get this feeling – even though he was sitting right next to me – that he had already vanished and I'd somehow missed it. That he hadn't gone through the wall, but had just evaporated where he sat, thinly exiting a life he didn't know how to live anymore.

Cam was quieter than I'd ever seen him. And worried. I'd never seen him so worried. If he didn't believe us before about the wall, he believed us now. He bit his fingernails as he looked at it and it was like he was watching the most suspenseful movie he'd ever seen in his life. The voices were back now, too, and even though it was hard to make out exactly what they were saying, it was pretty obvious that they were having a grand old time in there. There was a lot of yelling and laughing going on, carefree noises, the sounds of children being children. Only they weren't children, I kept reminding myself. They were the farthest thing away from being children that you could get.

It was late one night. Dad snored softly in his chair as Cam rubbed his own stubbled cheek. I was dying for a drink, thirsty in a way I didn't know I could be, and I could only imagine that Cam needed a little something to smooth out the edges, as well. He looked like he was about to come apart.

I caught his eye and motioned my head toward the stairs. He looked at Dad and shrugged.

"It's okay. He's out. He hasn't slept in days. He's not going anywhere. Besides," I said in a loud whisper, "we'll only be gone a minute."

Cam looked worriedly at Dad and then at the wall. Back and forth like that a few times and then I saw him kind of let go a little, watched his shoulders relax as he moved his hand away from his face.

"I guess we could take a break," he said. "But just for a minute. You promise, Vaughn?"

I got a little choked up when he asked me that, because I barely ever felt like the big brother in our relationship.

"Just for a minute!" someone in the wall shot back, clear as day. It sounded like it could have been Uncle Bert, but that's only because I had no idea who else was in there. How far the thing went back.

We slithered off to do our drugs in a shameful single-file,

shoulders slumped, and we weren't halfway up the stairs when we heard the sound. Kind of wet and hollow at the same time, it was a primordial noise, maybe even vaguely existential, like the sound of someone being born and realizing the futility of life at the exact same time.

We turned and sprinted back, but by the time we got there, Dad was already gone. And the only sign that he'd gone into the wall was a little dollop of what looked like quicksand in the spot where he'd gone in, as though the wall couldn't decide if it wanted to be liquid or solid. It shimmered for no more than a second and then was solid again.

It was bone-shatteringly silent for a second and then Cam threw himself against the wall.

He was howling, beseeching, indiscriminately making deals with the Devil and God despite knowing full well the non-compete in place between them.

I tried to pull him away, but he threw my arms off him. He was trying to speak through the tears, but it was hard to make out what he was saying at first, his sobs punctuating each word as though he were stopping to read a telegram in the Belle Époque. Finally, he calmed down enough that I could make out: "You...[SOB-SNIFFLE]...fucker...(SOB-HEAVE]take me...with...you!"

I didn't want to break it to him that in the natural order of things I would probably be the next to go. Eldest son, birth-rights, that kind of thing, so I just held him by the shoulders, tried to ease him away from the wall. He resisted and I was afraid to pull him too hard. Afraid that he would crumble in my hands, break apart like plaster or come away like dust.

I stood and leaned over him. Blood was dripping from the tips of his fingers and something small, slimy and bloody lay on the floor next to him. It took me a second to see that he'd torn a fingernail off from clawing at the wall.

"It's worse than dying," I said suddenly, surprising both myself and Cam.

He stopped crying, a little taken aback by hearing me raise my voice, which I barely ever did, and used the back of his hand to wipe away snot and tears.

"What is?" He looked up at me and for a moment he was a child again, my little brother, curious and a little bit afraid. It was easy to pity him like that, but I realized I pitied him already, maybe always had. Having our father as a role model was never going to end well.

"Going in there." I pointed to the wall, which was silent now, listening, I felt, waiting, maybe hoping to be shown the way out.

"But Dad…" he started to say, and I shushed him, waved the name away with a flick of my condescending wrist.

"It's worse than dying, because when you're gone…" I stared out the window in the kitchen door, looked past the lawn, the street, to our neighborhood and whatever lay beyond, the whole world, I guessed, but I'd have to find someone who could verify that, "…you're gone. But when you're in there," I pointed to the wall, "you're always alive, clawing your way through a hundred different versions of the same truth, a hundred different variations of the same story, and you never come to any agreements about anything and that's it. That's forever."

He stared at me, mouth hanging open, shocked maybe, but it also looked like fear. I could see that he was starting to feel in his bones what regret was really like, how far down it went.

Time passed. Slowly, but it passed, and I watched him as his breathing slowed down, as the tendons in his neck stopped trying to strangle him, as the sweat on his forehead started to evaporate. When it seemed as though he was in a better place I leaned down so that my face was right next to his.

"I'm going to go upstairs and get that bottle of whiskey. We're going to have a couple of drinks and then figure out what comes next. Because this..." I waved at the wall without even giving it the courtesy of a glance, "...doesn't have to be it."

Not waiting for him to answer, I gave his shoulder a little squeeze, and jogged up the stairs. I took a deep breath when I got to the top, grabbed the bottle off my dresser, and by the time I got back down, I saw the tips of his toes disappearing into the wall.

"Fuck," I said to no one in particular, shaking my head at the puddle in the wall that shimmered for a moment and then was gone.

I sat heavily in the old chair, poured myself a glass, and drank it off in one monumental swallow. I'd forgotten to make a toast,

I thought, pouring myself another so as not to be gauche, and held it aloft, saluting first the wall and then the door.

I thought about it for awhile before finally landing on "Fuck!" again, drinking it down to its nothingness. I refilled my glass, hoisted it, and repeated the toast, because I felt like it bore repeating. "Fuck!"

A din grew from inside the wall and I left the room, feeling pity for those poor sounds that had no idea what they wanted to be. I'm sure there was some laughter, some tears, some praying, maybe a scream or two, but all together…what a sad way to come to nothingness.

I wandered into the living room and picked up the tune my father had tried to sing earlier. It was a song I knew well, actually. I'd heard Mom sing it a thousand times cooking in the kitchen, folding laundry, running errands. Always working for us and never asking anything in return. Just her and that little voice that ached to be heard.

Humming, I strolled around, another full glass in my hand, touching my family's things, letting my fingers slide over the generations of books, pictures, and furniture I already knew I wouldn't keep. Except…

Along the bookcase, in between the *G* and *H* volumes of the *Encyclopedia Britannica*, I slid out a 45 record. I pulled it from its sleeve, blew the dust from its oily surface, and put it on the record player, which surprised me by working. I lowered the needle and it crackled to life like old knees in the morning. At first nothing but the dull hiss of white noise, and then…a string quartet, a saxophone, instruments building one on top of the other, soaring, until it felt like there was no room for anything else. That it was as high as it could go and to go any higher would bring it all down.

I turned up the volume and danced through the living room, across the den, and back into the kitchen, the music tailing me like a shadow. I hummed along, my eyes closed, felt it swirl within me as I moved my hand in the air in front of me, conducting what came after infinity.

The noise from the wall had stopped, but I pretended not to notice. I swayed and sang, stopping only to take little sips of whiskey, and I could feel them in there, listening to the song and my voice. I felt their need in that stillness, an ache I almost understood. I could feel that they wanted to sing along and soar to those heights. Now that it was too late, they wanted to know how the song went, and the truth of the matter was, I would have gladly told them. All they ever had to do was ask.

About the Author

Adam Greenfield is the author of two novels, *Circa* and *Mountain Lion Blues* (both published by Pelekinesis). He lives in Los Angeles with his wife and two daughters.

BAMBOO DART PRESS

112 N. Harvard Ave. #65

Claremont, CA 91711

chapbooks@bamboodartpress.com

www.bamboodartpress.com

www.ingramcontent.com/pod-product-compliance
Lightning Source LLC
Chambersburg PA
CBHW080824120626
46556CB00010B/3389
9781962316033